DEDICATION

To Mike, Steve, Jim, Eric,
and Dan... the FUNATIX!

--P.L.

# Book Two: Off-Season

a graphic novel by

## Jim Lawson
and
## Peter Laird

CREATED BY **JIM LAWSON** and **PETER LAIRD**

STORY BY **JIM LAWSON** and **PETER LAIRD**

PENCILS BY **JIM LAWSON**

INKS BY **JIM LAWSON** and **PETER LAIRD**

LETTERING BY **PETER LAIRD**

COVER PAINTED BY **MICHAEL DOONEY**

**PLANET RACERS™: BOOK TWO / "OFF-SEASON"**
Published by Zeromayo Studios LLP
P.O. Box 417, Haydenville, MA 01039
www.planetracers.com
™ and Copyright © 1998
Zeromayo Studios LLP

Printed in Canada.

First Printing, August 1998

ISBN 0-9661985-1-4

# Synopsis of the first PLANET RACERS graphic novel, PLANET RACERS BOOK ONE: "Life Cycle"

Halfway through the Planet Racing championship series of 2999, a terrible accident almost ends the brilliant career of the talented but egotistical open-class racer Godman Falcon, the Koyoshada factory's "Golden Boy". Falcon was number two in the series points, in a heated rivalry with Tripper Nitro, his teammate on the Koyoshada factory team.

But the accident, which was precipitated by Godman stopping on the race track and doing a burnout in frustration over narrowly losing the race to Tripper Nitro, changed everything. The pilot of the bike which crashed into the back of Falcon's machine died... and Falcon narrowly avoided prosecution. His cushy job as a factory racer was over.

Enter Methania Fitts. Having recently fired her pilot, the Zip-addicted Jahr Neiomaze, this scrappy Massey-Basheene team leader and navigator offers the disgraced Godman Falcon a spot on her privateer team. Her quick temper and his prima-donna nature make for some prickly confrontations, but as the season progresses, they start to trust each other and come together as an effective racing team.

**GODMAN FALCON**

**TRIPPER NITRO**

Meanwhile, Jahr Neiomaze spies on Godman and Methania, his anger at being kicked off Team Fitts festering. He, in turn, is watched by the prognosticating mega-computer, Janus — a cybernetic oracle designed and built at huge expense by the Toyetsu Corporation, primary competitor of Koyoshada. Janus was created to take in and process vast amounts of information, seeing connections and structures impossible for any humanoid to perceive, allowing it to predict the future and see into the past with remarkable accuracy.

Jahr's rage boils over during the two-day race on Edenior-3, when he attacks Methania and Godman in their camp. Jahr leaves only when Methania threatens him with a flare gun. Making a connection to buy some Zip, Jahr steals from his dealer a Toyetsu security passcard. Thinking he can find the dealer's Zip stash, Jahr enters Toyetsu's corporate building on Endenior-3, and is quickly discovered, captured, and interrogated.

Something goes wrong during the interrogation, and Jahr is seemingly lobotomized. But while Methania and Godman are battling to a remarkable first place finish in the race on Edenior-3, Jahr's now-mindless husk is reanimated by the guiding consciousness of Janus, to do Janus' bidding.

**METHANIA FITTS**

While the Planet Racers move on to the next race venue — a fantastic buried megatropolis on Dosmarranna — the Janus-driven Jahr Neiomaze golem moves in mysterious ways, collecting various pieces of hardware... and Toyetsu begins to see that something is wrong with Janus. Toyetsu dispatches their operative Mr. Zoneatore, working in concert with the most powerful mobile computing unit ever made — LW666, the "Lone Wolf" robot — to discover the meaning of Janus' connection to the former Planet Racer Jahr Neiomaze.

The race on Dosmarrana is disrupted by the awakening of an ancient defense grid which wreaks havoc on the racers, and ends with an uncharacteristically selfless act by

**JAHR NEIOMAZE**

Godman Falcon wherein he sacrifices the Fitts Racing machine to save the lives of some competitors, the Quazine national race team.

But every cloud has a silver lining. Godman's actions win him praise, and the Quazines offer Team Fitts their racing machine from the previous season. In spite of Godman's protests (for some reason, he just doesn't like or trust the Quazines), Methania accepts, and Team Fitts manages to retrofit the Quazine machine in time for the last race of the season on Basfornia, site of the mysterious living Malkrill Sea.

Mr. Zoneatore and Lone Wolf figure out what Janus/Jahr are up to -- they are building a hyperdense archival storage unit with which to transfer the core of Janus's electronic soul into the immense storage systems of the Tarkov array, the galaxy's largest foldspace communications center -- which is situated on Basfornia! Zoneatore sees that swift action is critical -- if Janus' consciousness is allowed to enter the foldspace com net, it can never be eradicated, short of shutting down the array, and that is as unlikely as to be impossible.

On the shores of the Malkrill Sea -- a living soup inhabited by trillions of trillions of tiny organisms, the malkrill, which some scientists believe to be somewhat telepathic -- the final race begins. Zoneatore and Lone Wolf corner Jahr, just as he is about to connect Janus to the array. Jahr escapes, disabling Lone Wolf in the process, and chaos ensues on the race track as Jahr once more attacks Godman and Methania, this time as they are speeding along toward the finish line. At a critical moment, as the Fitts bike catches some big air over an inlet of the Malkrill Sea, a desperate blow from Godman dislodges Jahr, who falls to his doom into the Malkrill Sea, where his body is devoured by the malkrill.

An amazing fifth place finish by Team Fitts puts them into third place in the championship, while Godman Falcon's ex-teammate Tripper Nitro and the Koyoshada team take first place. Godman and Methania celebrate their good fortune, and Godman surprises Methania by asking to stay on her privateer team.

And in the warm darkness of the Malkrill Sea, the true intent of Janus is realized. Janus never intended to transfer its consciousness into the Tarkov array -- that was an effective misdirection on its part, to mislead its enemies. Instead, the seed of Janus' consciousness was stored within Jahr Neiomaze's brain, and when his body was devoured by the malkrill, Janus' consciousness became part of this vast ocean of tiny minds, all linked telepathically... and now all controlled by a greater organizing mind -- that of Janus. For now, Janus' ultimate purpose remains a mystery...

**MR. ZONEATORE**

**QUAZINES**

**"LONE WOLF" ROBOT**

**MALKRILL**

# PLANET

# RACERS

## *CHAPTER*

## *ONE*

ZEK

3

... ONCE AGAIN, *TRANS-SYSTEMS SPACELINES* WOULD LIKE TO *THANK* YOU...

MR. FALCON? MAY I GET YOU A *DRINK*, OR SOMETHING TO *EAT*...?

HUH? YEAH, ELANTRA, I COULD *USE* A DRINK...

... GIMME A DOUBLE GURTANGY SNAPBOOZLE, PLEASE.

BEEN ONE OF THOSE DAYS, MR. FALCON...?

FEELS MORE LIKE *TWO* OF THOSE DAYS... THANKS.

... FOR TRAVELING ON THE *NEUTRON QUEEN*. THE PILOT HAS JUST INFORMED ME THAT WE HAVE EXITED *FOLDSPACE*. STASIS BUFFERS ARE *OFF*, AND YOU MAY NOW *MOVE* ABOUT THE CABIN.

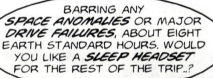

HOW LONG BEFORE WE ARRIVE AT PALLADIES NUVA?

BARRING ANY *SPACE ANOMALIES* OR MAJOR *DRIVE FAILURES*, ABOUT EIGHT EARTH STANDARD HOURS. WOULD YOU LIKE A *SLEEP HEADSET* FOR THE REST OF THE TRIP..?

NO THANKS...

... I THINK I'D BETTER STAY *AWAKE*.

7

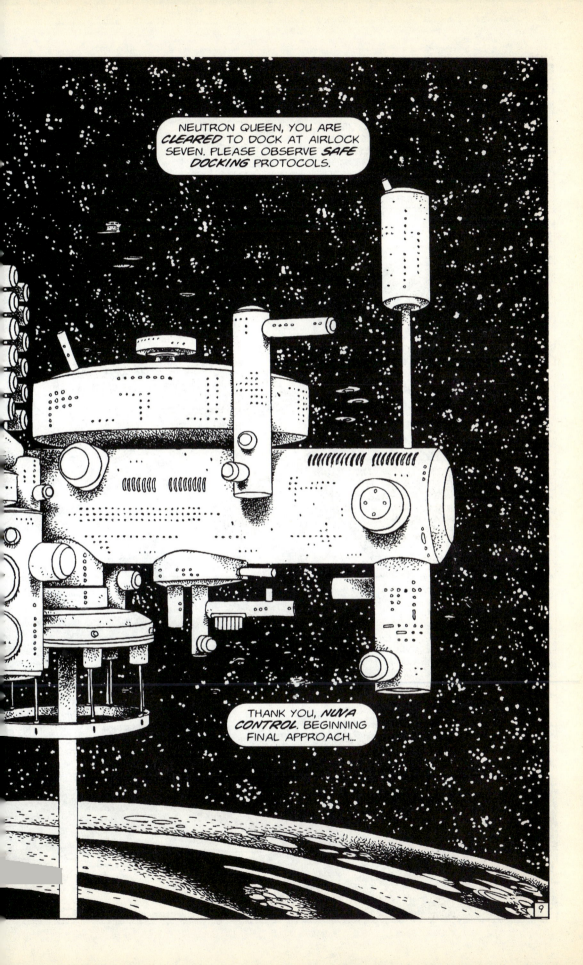

25

NO *WONDER* HE DIDN'T *COMPLAIN* ABOUT CARRYING MY LUGGAGE ALL THAT WAY! HEY, THANKS, PROOT... YOU'RE *OKAY!*

UH... I *DID* COMPLAIN... BUT... YOU'RE WELCOME! IT'S THE *LEAST* I COULD DO FOR MY COUSIN'S RACING *PARTNER!*

SO, METHANIA... THIS IS THE *GREAT* GODMAN FALCON...

MUEN...!

*ANOTHER* RELATIVE, METH?

*HUH!* YOU COULD SAY THAT, *HUMAN.*

UH... GODMAN... THIS IS *MUEN.* HE'S..

# PLANET
# RACERS
## *CHAPTER*
## *TWO*

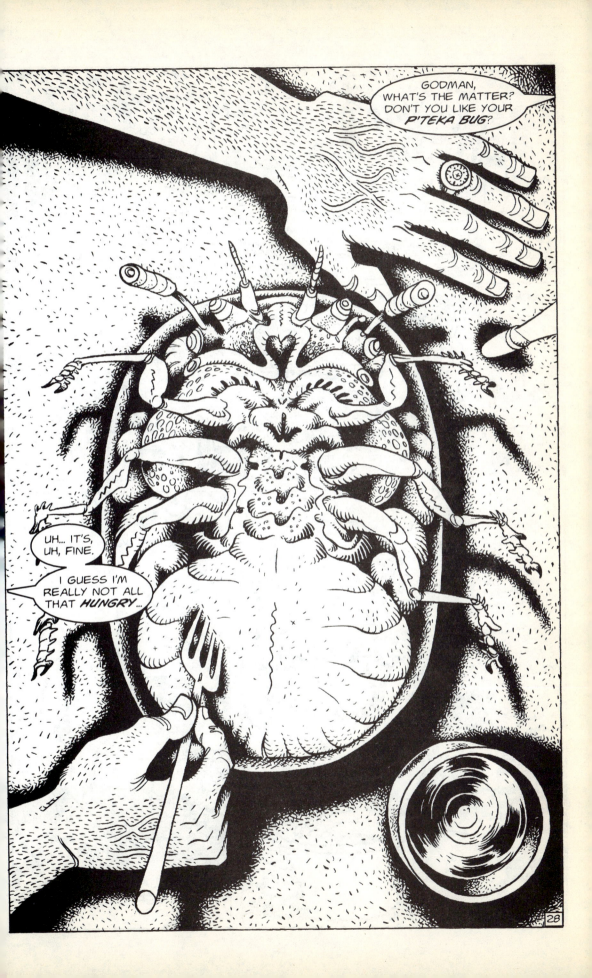

YOU'RE PROBABLY RIGHT. IT'S JUST THAT MUEN AND I... WELL, WE HAVE SOME *ISSUES* WE HAVE TO WORK OUT...

... AND IT'S *HARD* FOR ME TO TALK ABOUT IT.

BUT THAT'S MY OWN PERSONAL STUFF -- IT'S NOTHING FOR *YOU* TO WORRY ABOUT. AND THERE ARE OTHER, *BIGGER*, PROBLEMS FOR ME HERE...

SUCH AS...?

THINGS HERE ARE A LITTLE.. *TENSE*.

WHAT DO YOU MEAN?

YOU KNOW THAT FOR THE MASSEY-BASHEENE, RIDING SKILLS ARE LIKE AN EXTENSION OF OUR *RELIGION*...

... AND THERE ARE *MANY* AMONG OUR TRIBE WHO FEEL THAT ANY *COMMERCIAL EXPLOITATION* OF THOSE SKILLS...

... IS AN *AFFRONT* TO THE SPIRITS OF BALANCE, WHICH WE *REVERE*. MY DECISION TO PURSUE A RACING CAREER HAS PUT *ALL* OF MY FAMILY IN A DIFFICULT POSITION.

*DAMN!* TALKING ABOUT THIS REMINDS ME OF WHY I WANTED TO GET THE *HELL* OUT OF HERE...!

ANYWAY...

...WE'VE GOT *WORK* TO DO. WANT TO SEE THE BIKE?

AND LEAVE MY STEAMED P'TEKA BUG? WELL... IF WE *HAVE* TO...

30

31

RIGHT... WE'RE TESTING INITIALLY WITH FRONT *AND* SIDE MOUNTED RADS...

...IF *THAT* DOESN'T SOLVE THE PROBLEM, WE'VE GOT A FEW OTHER IDEAS.

HEY, WHAT'S *THAT*?

WE CALL IT *L'LEIL'S ASCENT*. THE POLESTEPS LEAD UP AND AROUND TO THE TEMPLE AT THE TOP.

OUR *MALES* CLIMB THE STEPS AS A *TEST* OF SKILL AND BALANCE.

IS IT HARD TO DO?

FROM WHAT I *HEAR*, YES... VERY HARD.

YOU'VE *NEVER* CLIMBED UP THERE...?

WOMEN AREN'T *ALLOWED* UP THERE... BUT WE HAVE OUR OWN "COMING-OF-AGE" TRIAL IN THE *CAVE OF V'TOR*.

YEAH? WHAT'S THAT LIKE?

IMAGINE TIGHTROPE-WALKING *BLINDFOLDED* OVER OPEN *LAVA* PITS WHILE CARRYING IN EACH HAND AN OPEN VESSEL OF *SACRED* YET VIRULENTLY *TOXIC* OIL WHICH MUST *NOT* BE SPILLED...

YEAH..?

THAT'S THE *EASY* PART.

OH...

HERE'S THE GARAGE...

32

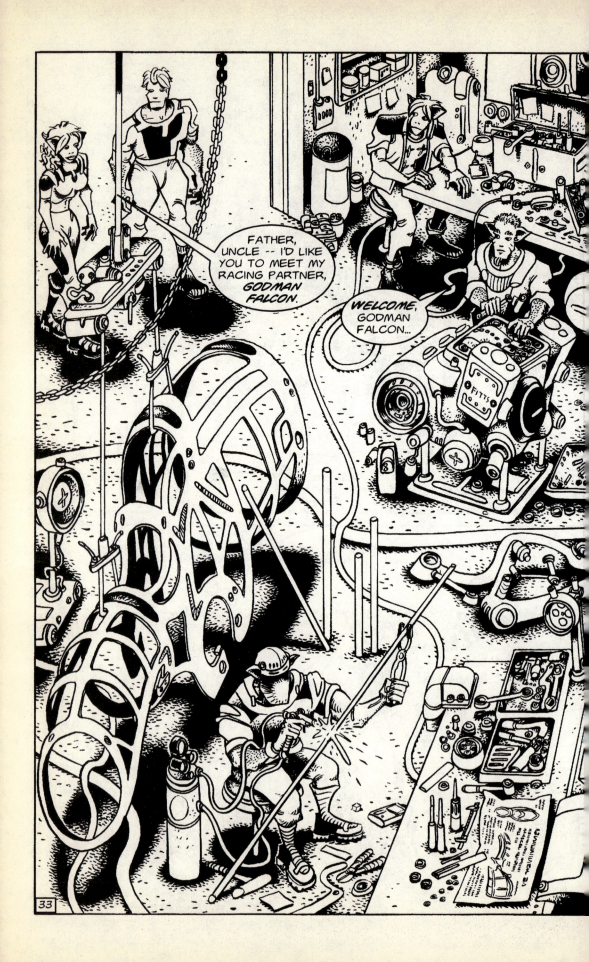

34

35

36

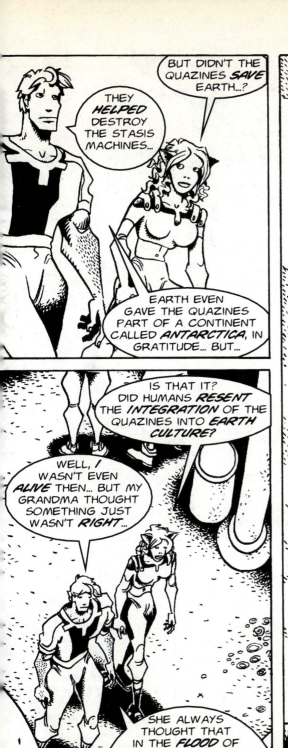

BUT DIDN'T THE QUAZINES *SAVE* EARTH...?

THEY *HELPED* DESTROY THE STASIS MACHINES...

EARTH EVEN GAVE THE QUAZINES PART OF A CONTINENT CALLED *ANTARCTICA*, IN GRATITUDE... BUT...

IS THAT IT? DID HUMANS *RESENT* THE *INTEGRATION* OF THE QUAZINES INTO *EARTH CULTURE?*

WELL, *I* WASN'T EVEN *ALIVE* THEN... BUT MY GRANDMA THOUGHT SOMETHING JUST WASN'T *RIGHT*...

SHE ALWAYS THOUGHT THAT IN THE *FLOOD* OF SIMULTANEOUS *ANGER* AT WHOEVER *PLANTED* THE STASIS GENERATORS, AND *GRATITUDE* TOWARD THE QUAZINES FOR HELPING GET *RID* OF THEM, HUMANS OF THAT TIME...

... *MISSED* SOMETHING... SOMETHING *IMPORTANT*. IT WAS ALL JUST TOO... *NEAT.*

AND MY EXPERIENCE HAS SHOWN ME...

"... THINGS RARELY WORK OUT THAT WAY."

THERE THEY ARE...

*THAT'S* THE FALCON?

HE DOESN'T LOOK LIKE *MUCH*...

DON'T *UNDERESTIMATE* HIM, BEX. FOR A HUMAN..

38

... HE SEEMS TO HAVE THE *GODS'* FAVOR.

AND METHANIA? DOES HE HAVE *HER* FAVOR, TOO...?

CAREFUL, BEX... YOU KNOW THAT'S A SORE SUBJECT.

SORRY... IS SHE STILL STAYING AT HER FATHER'S...?

YES, DAMN IT. AND WE HAVEN'T BEEN TOGETHER... AS *MAN* AND *WIFE*... SINCE SHE'S COME BACK.

MUEN, MY FRIEND... THIS DOES *NOT* SOUND GOOD. DO YOU THINK SHE WILL TRY FOR AN *ANNULMENT*?

HUH! I'M *CERTAIN* OF IT.

AND... WILL YOU *CHALLENGE* HER?

...

YES... YES, I WILL.

YOU SOUND PRETTY *WOBBLY*, MUEN. ARE YOU SURE OF THIS COURSE?

YES! I -- I *HAVE* TO CHALLENGE HER!

I SHOULD HAVE MORE STRONGLY *OPPOSED* HER DECISION TO GO AND DO THIS *FOOLISH* RACING THING... BUT I DIDN'T. NOW I HAVE TO *CORRECT* THAT ERROR.

S-SORRY, FATHER. I'LL CLEAN IT UP RIGHT AWAY...

YES, DO... SIGH...

THE SPIRITS OF BALANCE HAVE *NOT* BLESSED THAT BOY...

HEY, IT'S COOL, PROOT -- EVERYBODY HAS A *KLUTZ* MOMENT NOW AND THEN...

EVERY *HUMAN*, PERHAPS... BUT WE ARE *MASSEY-BASHEENE.*

SO, FALCON... DID METHANIA MENTION THAT TOMORROW IS OUR FIFTH WEDDING ANNIVERSARY?

NOPE...

...SHE ONLY TELLS ME ABOUT THE *IMPORTANT* STUFF.

UH... GODMAN...

... IT'S NOT *EASY* TO BE MARRIED TO ONE WHO IS *AWAY* MOST OF THE YEAR.

WITH ALL OF THE TIME METHANIA... *WASTES*... ON RACING *OFFWORLD*, IT IS AS IF WE'VE BEEN MARRIED ONLY ONE OR TWO YEARS.

*WHAT?* WHAT DID YOU *SAY* --?!

LONG ENOUGH...

KNOCK KNOCK

AH... AN *OPPORTUNE* INTERRUPTION...

42

43

I *SUSPECT* THE COUNCIL WISHES TO DISCUSS OUR *INVOLVEMENT* WITH METHANIA'S RACING EFFORTS.

HRRR! THEY INTEND TO *FRY* US!

DON'T *OVERDRAMATIZE*, DHUPA. WE DON'T KNOW YET *WHAT* EXACTLY THEY WANT.

WISHFUL THINKING, DHUPA... YOU'VE SEEN, AS WELL AS I, THE *DISAPPROVING* LOOKS FROM OUR NEIGHBORS. WE'LL GET *LITTLE* SUPPORT THERE.

MAYBE... MAYBE WE CAN DEMAND A *REFERENDUM*...

THEN IT'S *OVER*, L'EIL DAMN IT!

WE'LL KNOW MORE TOMORROW. FOR NOW, I STILL HAVE SOME TRANSMISSION GEARS TO RECUT.

I'LL SEE YOU AT THE DYNO RUN TOMORROW MORNING. GOOD NIGHT.

HRRR... TOMORROW...

YES... *TOMORROW!*

44

NEXT MORNING...

ArENA

BBRRAAAPPPP!

YAHHH--!

SCRREECH!

CHK

45

SHOULDN'T *WALK* IN THE *RIDNG BOWL*, HUMAN...

...IT CAN BE... *DANGEROUS.*

YEAH.. I MIGHT GET RUN OVER BY SOME *ASSHOLE*...

SO...

...HAS SHE *ASKED* YOU?

HAS **WHO** ASKED ME **WHAT?**

METHANIA... MY WIFE...

HAS SHE ASKED YOU TO **CHALLENGE** ME?

WHAT, FOR **DORK** OF THE YEAR? NO CONTEST, MUEN...

... **YOU** WIN.

SO... METHANIA HAS NEGLECTED TO TELL YOU OF THE **CINOCONPARTA**...?

APPARENTLY THERE'S A **LOT** OF STUFF SHE'S NEGLECTED TO TELL ME... WHAT IS IT?

OUR **TRIBAL** TRADITIONS ALLOW AN **UNHAPPY** PARTNER A CHANCE TO LEAVE A MARRIAGE, ON THE FIFTH WEDDING ANNIVERSARY. EITHER PARTY MAY CHOOSE TO **RENEW** OR **RETRACT** THEIR VOWS... WITH CERTAIN... **SANCTIONS.**

I GET IT...

... **DIVORCE,** MASSEY-BASHEENE STYLE.

MORE **CIVILIZED** THAN YOUR HUMAN WAY... BUT **ROUGHLY** EQUIVALENT.

SO... YOU'RE SAYING... METHANIA WANTS **OUT**...?

FOR ALL INTENTS AND PURPOSES, RACING HAS **TAKEN** HER FROM ME, FALCON. NOW, SHE WISHES TO MAKE IT **OFFICIAL.**

46

HUH... BUT I DON'T GET THIS *CHALLENGE* THING.

THE UNHAPPY PARTY MAY CHOOSE TO CHALLENGE THE OTHER TO A *RACE*...

... OR THEY PICK A *THIRD* PARTY TO RACE FOR THEM. THE WINNER DETERMINES THE *DISPOSITION* OF THE CINOCONPARTA.

WHEW... SOUNDS COMPLICATED.

CAN'T YOU JUST SHAKE HANDS AND SAY GOODBYE...?

FOR ALL HER *FRUSTRATNG* IDIOCYNCRACIES, METHANIA FITTS IS A *UNIQUE* WOMAN... AND WIFE.

IF *YOU* WERE IN *MY* SHOES...

...WOULDN'T YOU *FIGHT* TO KEEP HER?

47

48

# PLANET RACERS

## CHAPTER THREE

WHAT ABOUT THE WIRING?

UH... THAT WIRING DIAGRAM IS PRETTY *CONFUSING*... I RAN WHAT I COULD FIGURE OUT TO THE MAIN SERVICE... LEFT THE REST FOR THE *EXPERTS*.

MEANING *ME*. THANKS.

NO PROBLEM. WHAT ABOUT THE GYRO BACK-UP CIRCUITS?

THE *MAINS* AREN'T INSTALLED YET... SO LET'S *WAIT* TO CONNECT THE BACKUPS.

YEAH... EASIER TO *CALIBRATE* THAT WAY. WELL... ANYTHING ELSE I CAN DO? MAYBE HELP YOUR DAD...?

UM... I DON'T THINK SO, GODMAN...

... HE KIND OF PREFERS TO WORK *ALONE*, ESPECIALLY WHEN HE'S UNDER *STRESS*. BESIDES, PROOT'S AROUND IF HE NEEDS A HAND.

OH, I ALMOST *FORGOT* -- MUEN CALLED FOR YOU A COUPLE OF HOURS AGO.

FOR *ME*...? I WONDER WHAT HE WANTS...

51

52

YEAH, YEAH... MUEN TOLD ME ALL ABOUT IT THIS MORNING.

OH... WELL, I SHOULD TELL YOU -- I'M GOING TO *CONTEST* THE MARRIAGE.

HUH.

DID YOU TELL *MUEN* ABOUT THIS?

NO... BUT I THINK HE *KNOWS*.

"I THINK HE KNOWS"... GEEZ...

DON'T YOU THINK TWO PEOPLE WHO ARE *MARRIED* SHOULD *DISCUSS* STUFF LIKE THIS?

I KNOW, I KNOW... *NONE* OF MY BUSINESS. WELL... I'M OFF ON A *BUG HUNT*. SEE YOU LATER!

53

54

55

WHAT THE HELL ARE *THOSE* THINGS --? TELL ME WE'RE *NOT* GONNA *EAT* THEM...

*BOREPEDES*... NO GOOD. TOO *TOUGH* TO CHEW... NOT TO MENTION *TOXIC*.

OUR GAME IS FURTHER AWAY... AS THE SUN GETS *HIGH*, THE P'TEKA RETREAT TO THE *DEEP* ROCK.

UH-HUH... EXACTLY *HOW* MUCH FURTHER...?

HUH! YOU HUMANS DON'T HAVE MUCH *STAMINA*, DO YOU?

HEY, *PAL*...

... I GOT STAMINA UP THE *WAZOO!* I GOT SO MUCH STAMINA I DON'T KNOW WHAT TO *DO* WITH IT! I --

*QUIET!*

57

WATCH... AND *LEARN*...

HAH! ONE STROKE TO FLIP THEM OVER...

...AND ONE TO *STICK* THEM. SEE?

UH... YEAH...

*FLUID* MOTIONS -- THAT'S THE SECRET... THEY'RE *SKITTISH* CREATURES.

HERE -- YOU'LL NEED A '*TEKA BELT*' FOR YOUR CATCH. READY...?

WELL... I GUESS...

59

61

63

-- OUR *LENIENCY* IN THESE SANCTIONS IS AN ACKNOWLEDGEMENT OF YOUR FAMILY'S *IMPORTANCE* AND HONORED *STATURE* IN OUR TRIBE.

IT WOULD BE *UNWISE* OF YOU TO FURTHER *JEOPARDIZE* THAT STANDING.

NOW... TO THE NEXT MATTER -- THE *CINOCONPARTA* OF *MUEN ZOHN* AND *METHANIA FITTS*. BOTH PARTIES ARE PRESENT... STEP FORWARD TO THE BAR OF TRUTH.

TO THE *CONTINUANCE* OF YOUR UNION IN BALANCED *WEDLOCK*, HOW PLEAD YOU -- *YEA* OR *NAY*?

NAY.

*YEA,* HONORED ELDER... AND I CHALLENGE.

SO BE IT. METHANIA FITTS, AS ONE *CHALLENGED* IN THE CINOCONPARTA, YOU MAY CHOOSE A *CHAMPION*... IF YOU CANNOT FIND ONE TO *STAND* FOR YOU, YOU *FORFEIT* YOUR RIGHTS IN THE CINOCONPARTA.

I... I ASK TO STAND FOR *MYSELF*.

UH... EXCUSE ME, UH, YOUR, UH, HONOR... IF IT'S *OKAY* WITH METHANIA...

A *RADICAL* CONCEPT... COMING FROM A *FITTS*, IT'S NO SURPRISE. REQUEST *DENIED.*

BUT... I...

70

# PLANET RACERS

## *CHAPTER*

## *FOUR*

IT'S *MORE* THAN JUST MY MARRIAGE, NOW... BY *FORCING* THE ISSUE WITH MUEN, I'VE PUT MY FAMILY'S LIVELIHOOD IN *JEOPARDY*...

HUH? HOW SO?

THE RULES OF THE CINOCONPARTA ARE HARSH BUT *CLEAR*--

-- IF MUEN WINS THIS CHALLENGE, AND I *STILL* DON'T WANT TO CONTINUE THE MARRIAGE...

... HE HAS THE OPTION OF DEMANDING *COMPENSATION*.

WHAT *KIND* OF COM--

OH... I THINK I'M GETTIN' THE PICTURE...

EXACTLY. HE COULD TAKE HIS COMPENSATION FROM *ANY* OF MY FAMILY'S ASSETS.

... INCLUDING ALL THE *BIKE* STUFF...?

YES, L'LEIL *DAMN* IT!

SIGH... WHEN I DECIDED THREE YEARS AGO TO FIELD A TEAM IN THE PLANET RACING SERIES, I THOUGHT MY BIGGEST PROBLEMS WOULD BE GETTING *SPONSORS* AND *WINNING* RACES...

... I CAN'T BELIEVE HOW *NAIVE* I WAS... HOW OBLIVIOUS TO THE *CONSEQUENCES* OF MY ACTIONS...

... MY FAMILY, *SHUNNED* BY OUR TRIBE... MY MARRIAGE A *WRECK*...

... ALTHOUGH, *TRUTH* TO TELL, THAT MAY HAVE HAPPENED EVEN *WITHOUT* THE RACING...

AW, C'MON -- THAT MUEN'S JUST ONE BIG LOVEABLE *HUNK* OF --

GODMAN...

SORRY... LOOK, I KNOW YOU FEEL *GUILTY* ABOUT THIS... HELL, I WOULD TOO IF I KNEW THAT MY DECISION TO GO RACING HAD *SCREWED* MY WHOLE FAMILY...

THANKS... THAT'S *VERY* COMFORTING...

UH... THAT DIDN'T COME OUT RIGHT...

WHAT I *MEAN* IS, I DON'T THINK YOU WOULD HAVE BEEN *HAPPY* DOING ANYTHING ELSE...

... *REGARDLESS* OF THE CONSEQUENCES.

HMMM. AND ALL BECAUSE OF...

... JANUS. YES -- THE LOSS OF THE JANUS PROJECT WAS A TRUE DEATHBLOW TO THIS COMPANY.

EVEN *I* HAD NO REAL IDEA HOW *LEVERAGED* THAT PROJECT WAS. IT WILL TAKE THE SALES OF *ALL* OF TOYETSU'S ASSETS -- ALMOST LITERALLY DOWN TO THE BARE WALLS...

... TO COVER ALL OF OUR NOTES... AND OUR OTHER OBLIGATIONS.

ONE OF WHICH INVOLVES YOU, MR ZONEATORE... I ASSUME YOU ARE HERE FOR YOUR *PAYMENT*...?

ACTUALLY, I'M HERE TO *WAIVE* MY PAYMENT...

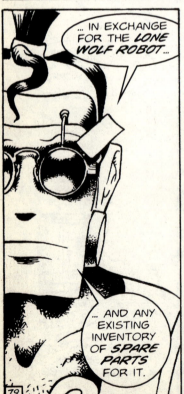

... IN EXCHANGE FOR THE *LONE WOLF ROBOT*...

... AND ANY EXISTING INVENTORY OF *SPARE PARTS* FOR IT.

A GENEROUS, THOUGH *CURIOUS,* OFFER, ZONEATORE. MAY I ASK...?

WITH *ALL* DUE RESPECT, BOMA... *NO.*

VERY WELL.

YOU HAVE A DEAL.

84

86

WHAK!

HAH!

KROKK!

THOMP!

UHHNH--!

YOU... FIGHT *WELL*... BUT YOU ARE *ADDLED*...

... FALCON IS NO RELATIVE OF MINE. I WAS REFERRING TO MY YOUNG COUSIN-IN-LAW, *PROOT*, THE MASSEY-BASHEENE. WHY ARE YOU AFTER *FALCON*?

KOFF... KOFF... IT'S... IT'S A LONG STORY.

YOU WON'T BE *GOING* ANYWHERE FOR A WHILE... WHY DON'T YOU TELL ME...

... IT MIGHT *HELP* ME DECIDE WHETHER I SHOULD TURN YOU OVER TO THE *AUTHORITIES*.

MY NAME IS *SEELA MORGAN*. GODMAN FALCON DELIBERATELY CAUSED A CRASH WHICH RESULTED IN THE *DEATH* OF MY *BROTHER*, CRITTER MORGAN...

HMM... I HEARD ABOUT THAT... BUT WASN'T IT *ACCIDENTAL*? AND WASN'T FALCON *CLEARED* OF ANY LIABILITY...?

PAH! *LAWYER'S* BULLSHIT AND CORPORATE *POLITICS*, THAT'S ALL THAT WAS. IT DOESN'T MATTER... I AM SWORN TO *AVENGE* MY BROTHER'S DEATH.

WELL... THAT WASN'T SUCH A *LONG* STORY...

DON'T MAKE *FUN* OF ME --!

I'M NOT! BY L'LEIL, YOU'RE *TOUCHY*...

I SUPPOSE I CAN'T GET IN THE WAY OF A DEBT OF *HONOR*...

...BUT I ALSO CAN'T LET YOU KILL FALCON *BEFORE* OUR RACE...

HAVE FALCON... BUT WAIT UNTIL AFTER I RACE HIM...

... THREE DAYS FROM NOW. AGREED?

AGREED. BUT *ONLY* THREE DAYS.

AFTER I *BEAT* FALCON IN THE CHALLENGE RACE, DO WHAT YOU *WILL*. IN THE MEANTIME...

... STAY OUT OF *SIGHT*, AND TRY NOT TO *KILL* ANYONE ACCIDENTALLY.

88

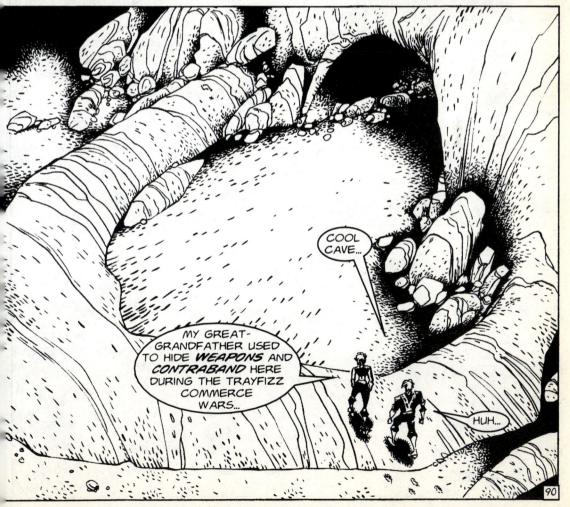

90

91

BUT... I DON'T GET IT...

... I THOUGHT YOU HAD TO TURN OVER THE *ENGINE* TO THE COUNCIL....

ER... YES...

WE GAVE THEM AN ENGINE -- THE *DEVELOPMENT* ENGINE....

*THIS* ONE... IS YOURS.

AREN'T YOU TAKING A BIG *RISK*?

A *MODERATE* RISK... BUT ONE WELL WORTH TAKING, I BELIEVE.

NO ONE OUTSIDE OF OUR FAMILY KNOWS OF THIS CAVE... BESIDES, THE BIKE'S NEARLY *DONE* -- NEXT WEEK WE'LL BE OUT OF HERE.

BUT... HOW...?

I HAVE *MANY* FRIENDS... IT WON'T BE TOO DIFFICULT...

... TO *SMUGGLE* THE BIKE OFFWORLD. WELL... WHAT DO YOU THINK?

I THINK...

92

# PLANET RACERS

## *CHAPTER*

## *FIVE*

SEELA! I HOPE YOU'RE NOT HERE TO --

DON'T *FRET*... I'LL *HONOR* OUR BARGAIN... I'M JUST HERE TO WATCH THE RACE.

HMMM... IS THAT *ALL*...?

WELL... I *DID* HAVE A QUESTION... ABOUT THE RACE...

YES...?

I KNOW WHY *YOU'RE* HERE... BUT I DON'T WHY *FALCON'S* RACING YOU... WHAT'S IN IT FOR HIM? WHAT'S HIS *ANGLE?*

HE'S DOING IT FOR METHANIA, I THINK ... OUT OF... *FRIENDSHIP.*

HUH! MORE LIKELY IT'S *SELF-INTEREST*... HE'S *SAVING* HIS *RIDE* FOR NEXT SEASON...

ARE YOU *SURE* ABOUT THAT?

UH...Y-YES, OF *COURSE* I AM. FALCON'S A SELFISH, UNTHINKING *BASTARD*...

...AND HE'S *RESPONSIBLE* FOR MY BROTHER'S *DEATH.* I *CAN'T* LET HIM GET *AWAY* WITH THAT.

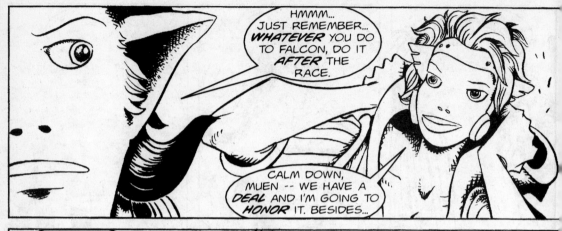

102

103

108

BRRAAAPP!

YEAH! WHOOH!

BRRPP!

BRAPP!

IF FATHER HAD SEEN ME DO THAT JUMP --!

SKRRCHH!

AHH... WHO AM I KIDDING? HE'D SAY IT WAS JUST LUCK....

114

# PLANET
# RACERS
## *CHAPTER*
## *SIX*

119

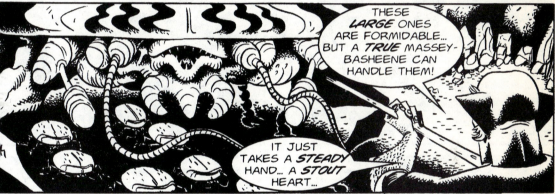

122

YEAH... *WAY* TOO SIMPLE FOR THE *GREAT* DHUPA FITTS TO THINK OF...

*WHAT?!* WHAT DID YOU *SAY*, BOY --?!

AW, JUST *FORGET* IT... LET'S JUST GET THE RACE BIKE BACK UP...

YES... THE RACE BIKE... PROOT, IN A *LONG* HISTORY OF DOING *STUPID* THINGS, AND DOING THEM *BADLY*...

... *THIS* HAS TO BE THE *WORST!* WHAT IN L'LEIL'S NAME WERE YOU *THINKING?!*

OH, BUT I *DO* UNDERSTAND -- YOU *EXIST* TO *TORTURE* ME!

YOU... YOU WOULDN'T UNDERSTAND...

THAT'S *IT!!!* FATHER, FOR SEVENTEEN YEARS I'VE LISTENED TO YOU *CRITICIZE* ME AND PUT ME *DOWN*...

"PROOT CAN'T BALANCE A THREE-WHEELER"... "PROOT IS AS FAST AS A ONE-LEGGED P'TEKA BUG"...

*WAKE UP!* I TOOK THE BIKE, *NOT* TO CAUSE PROBLEMS FOR YOU, BUT FOR ME... *FOR ME!*

I WANTED TO *PROVE* TO MYSELF THAT I COULD HANDLE THE BIKE... THAT I'M *BETTER* THAN YOU THINK I AM.

AND YOU KNOW WHAT? I WAS *WRONG!* I'M *NOT* THAT GOOD! BUT I FOUND IT OUT FOR *MYSELF*...

... *NOT* BECAUSE *YOU* SAID IT WAS SO. I'LL *NEVER* BE THE MASSEY-BASHEENE SON *YOU* WANTED, PERFECT BALANCE AND ALL THAT...

124

... BUT I DON'T *CARE*. I'VE SEEN THAT THERE'S *MORE* TO LIFE THAN *BALANCE*... AND I *CAN* DO THINGS RIGHT...

... LIKE *SAVING* US FROM THAT P'TEKA BUG -- *THAT* WAS PRETTY *GOOD*.

*PAH!* LUCKY... YOU WERE JUST *LUCKY!*

SIGH... YOU REALLY *DON'T* GET IT, DO YOU FATHER? THAT'S ALL RIGHT... I DON'T CARE *WHAT* YOU SAY ANYMORE. I'M *LEAVING*.

DON'T BE *STUPID*... IT'S A *LONG* WALK BACK...

IT'S NOT THE WALK BACK...

*WHAT!!!???!!*

... I MEAN I'M LEAVING THE *TRIBE*.

YOU'VE MADE IT *CLEAR* THAT I'LL NEVER AMOUNT TO *ANYTHING* HERE. I'M GOING *OFF-WORLD* WITH METHANIA...

... IF SHE'LL HAVE ME. SHE'S SHOWN ME THAT *FULFILLMENT* CAN BE FOUND *OUTSIDE* THIS TRIBE.

DON'T BE AN *IDIOT*, PROOT! SHE'S *RUINED* HER *MARRIAGE*... SHE'S ABOUT TO RUIN OUR *BUSINESS*...

SHE'LL RUIN *YOUR* LIFE, TOO. SHE'S A *DESTROYER!*

*NO*, FATHER. IF YOU WANT TO SEE THE *DESTROYER*...

... *JUST* LOOK IN YOUR *MIRROR*.

126

128

EXCUSE ME, SIR... BUT THAT WAS ONLY **THREE** RULES...

VERY **GOOD**, LONE WOLF. BEROGER'S FOURTH RULE IS "NEVER SAY MORE THAN YOU **HAVE** TO."

I SEE, SIR. IS THAT THE **HARDEST** RULE FOR **ORGANICS** TO FOLLOW?

UNFORTUNATELY, **YES**. AND IT'S TRUE FOR SOME **NON**-ORGANICS, AS WELL.

I'M NOT REFERRING TO **YOU**, OF COURSE, LONE WOLF... I FIND YOU TO BE MOST PLEASANTLY **PITHY**, AND **SPARE** WITH YOUR **VERBIAGE**...

THANK YOU, SIR.

NOW... BEFORE WE GO **FURTHER** -- DO A LEVEL THREE **SELF-DIAGNOSTIC** OF YOUR MEMORY CORE...

PROCESSING...

... I CAN DETECT NO **ERASURES** OR **GAPS** IN MY MEMORY FOR THE LAST 65.9873 DAYS.

... WHICH IS WHEN YOU WERE FIRST **ACTIVATED**. VERY GOOD.

PROCESSING...

THE PHENOMENA IN QUESTION ARE **MORE** THAN MERELY INTERESTING, SIR... THEY ARE **WITHOUT** RECORDED PRECEDENT.

THERE IS **NO** KNOWN EXPLANATION FOR THE FLOWING OF DEEP OCEAN CURRENTS TOWARD ONE CENTER...

NOW SCAN THE **INFOBLOK** I GAVE YOU EARLIER... WITH SPECIFIC ATTENTION TO THE NEWS ITEMS FROM **BASFORNIA**, AND THE REPORTS OF THE UNITED SYSTEMS PLANETARY SURVEY INSTITUTE.

YOU'LL NOTE SOME **INTERESTING** PHENOMENA, SPECIFICALLY IN THE **MALKRILL SEA**...

YES... **FASCINATING**, ISN'T IT? **SOMETHING** IS HAPPENING THERE... AND MY **GUT** TELLS ME IT HAS TO DO WITH **NEIOMAZE**... AND **JANUS**.

"THIS IS THE *TRUEST* TEST OF SKILL..."

"MUEN AND GODMAN HAVE TO KEEP THEIR *SPEED* UP... WHILE AT THE SAME TIME, *WHEELIEING* THROUGH THE NARROW GAP WITH THE FRONT WHEEL *CROSSED-UP*..."

"... THE *HANDLEBARS* OF THE BIKES BEING PURPOSELY MADE TOO *WIDE* TO FIT STRAIGHT THROUGH."

"THERE! MUEN HAS *ENTERED* THE GAP..."

METHANIA FITTS! YOUR HUSBAND, MUEN ZOHN, HAS **WON** THE CHALLENGE OF THE CINOCONPARTA...

... WILL YOU **RETURN** TO YOUR MARRIAGE?

...

NO.

VERY WELL! THAT IS YOUR **RIGHT**, UNDER THE LAWS OF THE CINOCONPARTA.

NOW YOU, MUEN -- IN THE EXERCISE OF **YOUR** RIGHTS AS WINNER OF THE CHALLENGE AND AS **SPURNED** MATE...

... WHAT **COMPENSATION** WILL YOU --

-- MFFPHT!

BLUTCH!

FALCON -- !

BRRRP!

SKRGH!

136

SEELA... EXCUSE ME FOR A MOMENT. DON'T GO AWAY...

I WON'T... I'M JUST GOING TO SIT DOWN... MY *HEAD* IS SPINNING...

HEY, MUEN...

FALCON...

"GODMAN".

GODMAN... YOU RACED *WELL*.

THANKS! HEY, I GAVE IT MY *BEST* SHOT...

HMMM... DID YOU...?

UH... WHATTYA MEAN? I WAS GOIN' *ALL OUT*... AND YOU KICKED MY *BUTT!* FAIR AND SQUARE, MUEN.

HMM... I SUPPOSE IT WOULD SERVE NO PURPOSE TO *ARGUE* THE POINT RIGHT NOW...

MUEN! I -- I DON'T KNOW WHAT TO SAY... BUT... *THANK YOU*.

I... SHOULD ALSO THANK *YOU*, METHANIA. YOUR *COMMITMENT* TO YOUR LIFE'S PATH HAS MADE ME... *RETHINK* SOME THINGS.

... AND WHILE OUR *MARRIAGE* DID NOT WORK OUT AS WE PLANNED, YOUR *FRIENDSHIP* IS MORE VALUABLE TO ME...

... THAN ANY *COMPENSATION* I COULD GET FROM YOUR FATHER'S BUSINESS.

WHAT WILL YOU DO NOW? HAVE YOU FOUND A RACE BIKE FOR NEXT SEASON?

WE'RE PETITIONING THE COUNCIL TO *RETURN* OUR ENGINE...

...AND IN THE *MEANTIME*, WE'VE MADE SOME, UH, *ARRANGEMENTS*...

138

140

... and now here's a sneak peek at the next PLANET RACERS graphic novel, "Janus Rising". This book is tentatively scheduled for release in late 1999, and will be approximately 300 pages in length.

DO A *CONTENT* SCAN. PARAMETERS: PLANET RACING, GODMAN FALCON, TRIPPER NITRO.

SCANNING...

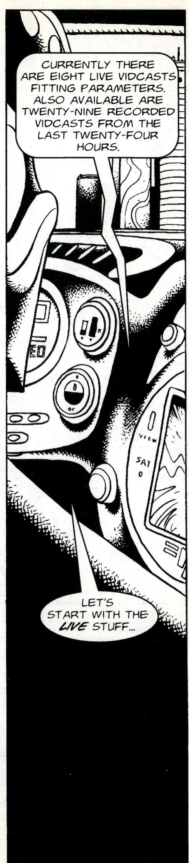

CURRENTLY THERE ARE EIGHT LIVE VIDCASTS FITTING PARAMETERS. ALSO AVAILABLE ARE TWENTY-NINE RECORDED VIDCASTS FROM THE LAST TWENTY-FOUR HOURS.

LET'S START WITH THE *LIVE* STUFF...

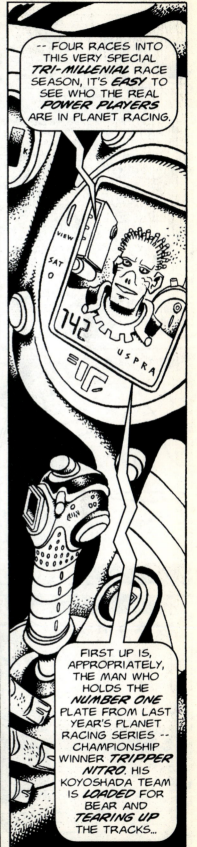

-- FOUR RACES INTO THIS VERY SPECIAL *TRI-MILLENIAL* RACE SEASON, IT'S *EASY* TO SEE WHO THE REAL *POWER PLAYERS* ARE IN PLANET RACING.

FIRST UP IS, APPROPRIATELY, THE MAN WHO HOLDS THE *NUMBER ONE* PLATE FROM LAST YEAR'S PLANET RACING SERIES -- CHAMPIONSHIP WINNER *TRIPPER NITRO.* HIS KOYOSHADA TEAM IS *LOADED* FOR BEAR AND *TEARING UP* THE TRACKS...

3

... WITH THREE *PODIUM* FINISHES -- INCLUDING TWO *WINS* -- KOYOSHADA IS ONCE AGAIN *NUMBER ONE* IN THE POINTS CHASE...

... FOLLOWED CLOSELY BY *TEMPORADO* AND THE *QUAZINE* NATIONAL TEAM, AS WELL AS THE HIGH-FLYING *GODMAN FALCON* OF THE FITTS RACING TEAM. FALCON, EX-TEAMMATE OF TRIPPER NITRO, HAS --

EXCUSE ME -- ONE MINUTE TO ZWEN HYPERDRIVE EXECUTIVE LOT ONE.

OKAY... TRACK AND RECORD *ALL* THE VIDCASTS FOUND IN YOUR SEARCH... AND *DOWNLOAD* THEM TO MY HOME VID SYSTEM...

... AND SEE IF YOU CAN GET ME A *TICKET* TO THE *NEXT* PLANET RACING EVENT.

SEARCHING...

WARNING! VEHICLE SHELL BREACHED! FLUID INTRUSION COMPROMISING CONTROL AND DRIVE SYSTEMS --

NOOOOO --! YAAAHHHH --!

DANGER! DANGER! RELEASE PERSONAL RESTRAINT SYSTEM IMMEDIATELY! FAILURE TO DO SO MAY RESULT IN TERMINATION BY INHALATION OF --

GLUB!

8

## BIOGRAPHIES

**Jim Lawson** graduated with a BFA in Illustration from Paier College of Art in New Haven, CT. He has worked as a writer/artist on the Teenage Mutant Ninja Turtles comic books, and as a designer of several figures and vehicles for the TMNT toy line.

Jim lives in western Massachusetts with his wife and three sons. His favorite activities include motorcycling and jetskiing.

**Peter Laird** has been a professional illustrator since 1976, a career he began shortly after graduating with a BFA in Printmaking from the University of Massachusetts in Amherst, MA.

In 1983 he co-created, with Kevin Eastman, the Teenage Mutant Ninja Turtles. PLANET RACERS is the most fun he's had with comics in a long time.

Peter lives with his family in western Massachusetts, not too far from Jim Lawson.

## ORDERING INFORMATION

PLANET RACERS BOOK ONE: "Life Cycle", the 276-page graphic novel by Jim Lawson and Peter Laird, is still available! Look for it at your local comics shop, or order direct from Zeromayo Studios. PLANET RACERS: "Life Cycle" is US $14.95 plus $5.00 shipping and handling (MA residents add 5% sales tax) per single copy.

PLANET RACERS BOOK TWO: "Off-Season" is available for $7.95 plus $3.00 shipping and handling (MA residents add 5% sales tax) per single copy.

Send check or money order to:
Zeromayo Studios, P.O. Box 417,
Haydenville, MA 01039.